Time

MACHINE

Daughter's Revenge

{ Noureen Jan }

Copyright © 2020 Noureen Jan

ISBN: 979-8-5733-2542-2

Time Machine

DEDICATION

Dedicated to my sister who is strong and mature person I have ever met, who always blow my mind with her comeback and one who taught me love and kindness. Thanks for believing in me and loving me unconditionally.

Hope you will like my book in which I have put my trust and faith. Always remember problems are never for forever, so take a moment for yourself, count the blessings you already have and be happy about it.

"She's a girl with the best intentions."

She's a girl with Great Personality.

Let me dedicate this Poem to you, my beloved sister:-

Never Underestimate her:-

*She handled everything no one else could, she
was what no one else would,
she grew humbler and stronger,
Where she was supposed to die,*

She was a lone warrior,
She won where no one else would,
She gave her heart, her soul,
And lost it all,
She survived what no one else could,
She was a miracle, everyone failed to
appreciate,
But she learned the stuff,
No one ever could.

She don't feel better at times,
Things don't go the way she expect,
Things change rapidly,
And so do the situations,
And so do she,
She runs after desires,
And forget the consequences after,
All those beautiful lashes,
Will turn into ashes,
What she sees doesn't exist,
What she avoid does,

Everything she achieve ends,
She know what lasts,
But she don't care if outcasts,

People talk only about future,
Nobody moves an inch,

"A kid by heart, a man by soul,
A poor giving alms and a rich crying for more, A
baby raised by maid, a woman left alone"

-Noureen Jan©

Time Machine

CONTENTS

NOTE:

(It's a short story, So, Chapter names are not involved.)

Time Machine

INTRODUCTION: TIME MACHINE

Erica steps out of her comfort zone and seeks revenge for her parents. She knows it's only she herself, no one is gonna come to help in such a chaos. As her parents are declared runaways and disappeared like they never existed. After all the suffering she bears, now her comeback scared her own grandmother. She was ready to take revenge and prove that something bad happened to her parents.

She left her house in New York, moved to Romania. Why Romania? There is this revenge what got her here! She might look innocent but she isn't! Well! Yes, that's what we can say! The intentions are not good, they are Evil. Trying to stay calm where she was supposed to be violent! Well, you will be thinking what is with her? So, here you go! I welcome you to her story or reality.

Where she meant a seducing boy, oh! No, correct that, a seducing gentle-man, Jake. Her life turned upside down being with him but there was something she was hiding. She caged her love for him; there was nothing she could have done about it. It was all her Revenge after all that lead her to him.

Well in her revenge she could do whatever was in power. She could even betray him. Let's leave him, there were so much more about her. She scarified herself to save parents and ended her life kind of. She proved that she loved, cared and was ready to do anything. She made her parents proud.

When she took her parents place and looked up to Jake who was crying, starring at her sadly and shockingly for the choice she made, she said, something in a painful voice, "I love you, Jake and nothing of this affected my love for you, not even my revenge, I wish I had one more day with you to explain why I did what I did and thank you for being there! It means a lot, Goodbye!

And then, Time-machine flashed, bright white light surrounded her and there she was gone.

Then, she suffered because of time that was repeating over and over again. It is stated that time heals everything, in her case, no; it didn't heal or changed but hurt more and more .She didn't have any hope of being rescued.

She never questioned herself if anybody will be able to save her after all the tragedies and illogical decisions. She didn't have any hope of being rescued. To reduce the pain, she tried to remember other happy moments of her life like her parents were alive now, moments shared with Jake, college days, childhood and all But No! She couldn't recall any of the memories but suffer the memory she was in.

Time Machine

PREFACE

This short story is written by me, Noureen Jan to let you enjoy the reality of Erica by replacing her by yourself and imagining whole in your mind. Erica is a strong girl and passionate about love and same time revenge. The story becomes more interesting and awesome when a reader imagines it. It's a power. Imagination is mental power that can move you to where you want to go. So, here, it was kind of motivation but the thing is "Your imagination is what makes you"

This story includes violence and love. The story scenes changes dramatically and emotionally. The characters are like they will leave you thinking! (Thinking what, you'll see.) The story avoids overlapping and ignores not to the point scenes. It sticks to the real (required) scenes.

As Erica, be passionate! Go ahead and read with imagination. So sit tight and read further..,

READY?

Let's take you into the painful yet happy ending story of Erica:-

Uncle came close, hugged me and asked, why? Erica? Why not me? I could have done it? I just hugged him back and whispered to him that it was time for a family reunion and his freedom as I had mine.

We heard sound, only 50 Seconds left. Everyone in the room panicked. Dad nervously asked what about the machine? To which I replied I got this dad. Mom asked what I meant by that. So, I went and took their place right before the time-machine.

I wanted the moment of me going to be fun and less painful. So, I tried to crack a joke but that didn't end well. I asked, dad? How you are so young and mom you look as gorgeous as always. Dad with tears in his eyes answered me because we were stuck in the same time for long period, so our body didn't grew any further and our mind was not able to release growth hormone.

Flashes of white bright light covered the room and there, I was frozen and captured by the time. It was nothing like frozen. As we know how powerful time is. It heals everything, changes almost everything. Well! I was stuck in a moment of my life where nothing healed and changed. My mind was sort of rewinding the memories of my birth. I could see my mom giving birth to me and I could see the pain she was going through and my dad by her side comforting Mom. I saw my mother's suffering and my father helpless. After few minutes, I was born. The happiness in the room was touching skies. My dad jumped with joy and sniff with relaxation while my mom was released of the pain, she saw me and burst into tears. Then, nurse put the baby that was me on my mom's chest. She looked at me like I was the precious thing she ever came across and had.

All of a sudden, the clock on the hospital wall ejected a sound like a roar; I looked up to it as it ticked anti-clockwise at high pace and after the coming of light, the moment ended. My mom was again suffering from the pain of birth. My dad trying to comfort her and then I was born. The time repeated itself. It was happening over and over again. I was trapped in this moment for how long Gods know. Well! That sucked for me. I couldn't complain. It was my choice. I made this decision of being trapped in the same moment.

Will anybody be able to save me after all the tragedies and illogical decisions? I didn't have any hope of being rescued.

(Oh! Wait, this is just the beginning of the story of Erica and really not the ending at least. Well! Let's see what actually happened, shall we? I welcome you to my story or maybe I can say my painful reality.)

STORY BEGINS:-
6 month ago (30/04/2019)

(I had my flight at night, so, it's good reached my destiny in the morning and get on already with my purpose.)

So, this is Romania, I have moved here to complete my education. In spite of education, why Romania? There is this revenge what got me here! I might look innocent but I am not! Well! Yes, that's what I can say! The intentions are not good, they are Evil. Trying to stay calm where I was supposed to be violent! Well, you will be thinking what is with me? So, here you go! I welcome you to my story or reality.

Hey, I am Erica Raines and have just moved to Romania to complete my studies as an effective excuse of coming here. My childhood was not easy, lost my parents when I was 8 years-old. Loved and raised by my Grandma. So, for fresh start, I am here! Choose to stay at Milton hotel. Completely, fascinated by the people here, they are kind and hospitality is just mind blowing. I am happy and excited to start my college days and live my life to the fullest.

So, in order to start over, I decided to join Weinberg Allen College, Famous College of the city. So, Today is Sunny! It looks like great day to get started with the purpose of coming in here, in Romania.

After getting ready, I had my breakfast, locked door and went straight to Weinberg Allen College. When I reached there, Confused where to go? I decided to ask someone there. So I approached watchman. He guided me to the administration block, while I was walking towards the block; I looked around, boys playing football, Couples making out, Flowers bloomed to their best. Okay! Now, I reached destiny, went inside, straight to the person responsible for new admissions, he handed me admission form, I filled the form, and did necessary formalities, and there all done! I took out my phone and called granny to let her know I did the admission. After having great conversation, I hung the phone.
I opened my phone and searched on N-maps app, and went to see the place. At one of the villa, I stopped, looked around carefully. Before i could rationalize things, I heard door opening, so I hid myself quickly, there was a man standing next to the door, it was clear, he was waiting for someone. I peeked and looked at the face of the man. Hmmm! So, he is Louka Serguis (in disgusted tone).
I carefully took a picture without being caught. Later, he was accompanied by someone, so, I left suspiciously. I opened chatting app namely I-chat, clicked on the chat above all, sent the picture and waited for the reply.

Next working morning, I had my breakfast and reached college by time, excited to make new friends. I was warmly welcomed and some students greeted me too in my classroom, everyone seemed nice and concerned except one. He was sitting alone, gazing outside the window, he was probably lost in his own world I called him queer one, maybe I was being judgmental, maybe he was an introvert, but what I felt was strange, I felt some close connection with that boy, my heart skipped a beat and started beating at high pace.
(I am not sure what that was? Like I don't know, I still have to figure that out myself first.)
So, I went to see where I can have seat. Yes! There she is sitting alone and reading some fantasy book as far as I could tell, let's say hi!
I greeted the girl but she was lost in the book, I cleared throat, ahem! Hello!
Reality hit her, Hi, I'm sorry. I was lost, sit!
I sat and we introduced each other, she was Nour Lincoln and I never thought she will become such a great friend. We were talking when teacher entered the classroom.
Well! Obviously, he introduced himself, he was our operation research teacher named Aaron Brown.
He in a calming tone, well!!!! It's a start of New Year of this college and I see new faces in the classroom, pointing towards me, please introduce yourself?
I definitely got up, started my introduction with I am Erica Raines from New York and all. While I noticed the queer one looking at me like he

knew me, I looked at him what I saw was unexpected, his eyes were full of tears about to pour down. I quickly changed my sight and sat down. In whole class, I was looking at him, he was tensed and I could tell he was in pain and was doing some calculations; something was not working out for him. After the OR class, he left. I didn't saw him for the rest of the day..

After college, I and Nour decided to go shopping. We enjoyed each moment together then we were off to our homes. I opened the door when my phone rang, it was Uncle.

He (in an aggressive tone) said, yes! The picture you sent is his. You are at the right place, dear. Stay away for a while until we come up with some effective plan. Understood?

I said nothing else, but yes and he hung up the phone.

Few days passed, Queer one was on leave, it was known that he was sick.

After few days, (One day was completely insane in college; I suppose you remember the queer one, right?)

I was with Nour and some other classmates when Jake joined us. (Queer one's name was Jake Winslow.) He looked surprised to see me and he greeted me like it was the first time. Everyone told him, is he okay? Because he not only confused me but everyone there as he told everyone he was seeing me for the first time. He left confused. We considered maybe he was sick, he doesn't remember. Day was normally spent.

Meanwhile, Uncle came up with the plan. So, I started planting my plan and get on with it as soon as possible. Days passed, Jake and I were getting close. So, this was not the intention of coming here, So, I halted the feelings right deep down in my heart. But he was Jake, until he gets what he wants he never stops.

He made me feel safe and heavens. He always took my side and stood by my side. He helped me with studying. He made my heart skip beats when he protected and cared for me. It was clear that I was falling for him as any girl in my shoe would have felt the same way.

Next Sunday, I was spying Louka Serguis to my best; I needed all the information about him, where he goes, who he meets, what jobs he was offering, so by any chance, I could enter his life and work my plan out.

I was about to make my move when Jake called, He wanted to meet. I answered by saying I was busy but what could have stopped me? I accepted my feelings, so did he! We were perfect couples. I went to see him, we made out in the rain till night. Later, I was scolded by my uncle as my relationship was coming between my missions. So, I told him in a serious way, I got it covered. I told him, it was my plan to be with him as he is the part of this plan.

Uncle in an angry voice, what? He knows? Are you out of your mind? It was supposed to be....

Before he could have said anything, I stopped him right there by saying before you say something else! Listen to me first! Jake is the adopted son of Louka Serguis. What could be the best way of getting into Louka's House and life except Jake himself? So, I went to see him yesterday, to make it look real.

Uncle in real voice said, how do you know that?

Well! The first day when I took the picture, I saw him right next to him when I left that place and I was surprised to see him as my batch mate. So, I came up with this plan. I otherwise did collect necessary information required!

"So? You decided to be in relationship with murderer's son? How does it make any of this right? See! We could have done it in any way but not this! Now! When you have done it? So, be done with everything of this and finish your purpose.

I in an agreed tone, Yes! Now, it's a piece of cake, covered too and I got it, no need to worry, I also want what you want, but I need your trust.

Uncle in calm way said, I trust you, dear! But I didn't know your plan so that's why I was angry. Now! Get on with this. You know, we can't talk hours, so, send me the required information. Be careful dear, Granny told me to tell you that she misses you and bye!

Yeah! Uncle, I will. You too take care and I miss everyone. See you, Bye!

I hung up the phone and sent information to my uncle through I-chat.

Next day, Jake wanted to introduce me to his father. Well! That worked out perfect for me as that's what i wanted from very beginning of this relationship. His father is a businessman who owns villa, luxurious cars and had fame. So, it was clear, revenge will not be easy to carry out.

Now, I was getting ready for meet up when door bell rang, it was Jake. He kissed me and we were both off to his villa. Outside door, he held my hand and asked if I was ready and I answered with, it was the moment I waited all these days! Gladly he said, Okay?! and kissed softly.

We entered the villa and went to see his father upstairs. We reached his father's room, he was probably busy. Jake told me to stay outside the room. To which I agreed. He went inside and had a little chit-chat with his father. While I was trying to peek inside and as far as I could tell, there were two bodyguards right next to the door. I wandered a little and Jake called for me.

I entered the room with a smile. So, his father greeted me with loving tone, and said so, you are the girl? I stood there without saying a word as I slightly looked at Jake. Jake knew I was nervous, so he answered in my place. Louka gave a little satisfying laugh and told me to relax!

He said, let's have dinner. I am hungry. To which Jake and I agreed.

While having dinner, Louka told us his marriage days and love story. To which I was surprisingly listening but deep down, I just wanted to grab the knife in fruit basket and slit his throat. The anger inside reached its maximum bearing point when he begin to talk about how he earned all the royalty and then it became hard for me to fake a smile, laugh, agreeing upon and everything.

But I couldn't help any of it, I had to sit there, I looked around and rationalized few things. He asked me about my parents, I answered in sadness yet revenge tone, I lost them when I was a kid. He looked at me suspiciously. After all what he has done, he must be suspicious to know more and more, he knows he can be busted. We had dinner, and after little more time I decided to say goodbye. Jake decided to drop me, on our way back, we talked, laughed on silly things. I asked him, did his father like me? To which he looked at me with his killing cute eyes and smile and then said, of course, he did!

(By the time, we reached the house, the moments I spent felt real and I wanted to live in that moment forever.)

We reached my home, when he came close and made my night by saying, I love you. To which I subconsciously answered with I love you too. We shared a moment.

(I know if I wouldn't have said, it's getting late, I should go now! that moment should have remained till dawn.)

I got out of the car and started walking towards

the door when he hurriedly got out of car and called for me, Erica? Wait! I stopped. He came close and kissed me deeply. I stepped back quickly. He looked surprised and begins to apologize.

(Deep inside me, it was clear I was really falling for him as I thought it was all about revenge. I shook my hand, and bend, have in the palm of hand and open my palm trying to think what to do?)

I raised my feet to reach his lips and kissed him. He grabbed my bag and was trying to search for something? I showed him my palm in which the keys of my house where hanging in the index finger.

I in a naughty tone! Searching for this? To which he picked me up and He opened the door then it was the night of roses, love and romance.

After few hours of sharing emotions, feelings and desires, I with half eyes open looked at the clock, it was late. I got up, and picked him up hurriedly, it's getting late, sorry! You can't stay here at night. So, you should leave.

Jake moans and said I want to stay! To which I definitely shoot him with serious look and he just got up and left the room. I followed him to the door, we kissed gently and he left. Now, I had a little time to myself, I tried to rationalize what I just did and thinking if I was supposed to do what I did? But nothing, all I remember was the moments we shared in the room. I went to the bathroom, washed my make-up off and went to bed while remembering. And, then decided to talk to my granny about what happened today, to get advice what to do next? But I already planned that if she says anything against it, I wasn't going to agree. I knew I had to fight for this relationship.

Granny said something that was unexpected, she didn't really judge me for my decision not because she loved me but it was my choice as she justified. She always supported me even in my childhood, she used to go against her own son for her grand-daughter. But she also declared that she would love to see Louka bearing for his crimes. To which I completely agreed.

Next day at college, Nour was happy when I told her about my relationship and yeah added that she keeps it a secret. Jake was playing football in the court, I sat there watching him with Nour and we talked. After the college, I and Jake reached my house, when I opened the door, my eyes were left wide open to see such a mess in the living room, things scattered around every corner of house. It looked like it was an unprofessional theft but to which Jake corrected me, nothing precious was stolen, not even gold, jewels, nothing. Jake called Cops, They investigated. When everyone left, I rushed to my room, moved the book shelf and opened the locker, and everything was clear now, my whole research on Louka was missing. So, I assumed someone knew who I really was and what my missions were! I hurriedly called my uncle, he suggested remaining calm and he would join me next day in the evening as it is becoming dangerous for me. He even scolded me and said it was my fault that I let Jake enter the house, the son of Louka.

I started receiving threats mails and message saying that I should break-up with Jake and stop whatever I was up to. I couldn't involve cops into any of this. I kept it even from Jake. And I was sure it was Louka.

(How hard it was for me to stay in this relationship, the more hard his father made for Jake. It was obvious Louka would have recognized me in the first place but maybe because of his son he kept quiet and said nothing and played along that meet-up night.)

Jake came to my hotel, and said in sad tone, "My

father is not ready to accept this relationship. He is forcing me to break-up with you."Then he added" I will not let him to ruin my relationship. He has no right to order or force me to break-up and do what he says, No! That can't happen. I can't leave without you, i want to grow old with you, have family, kids and everything with you by my side.

I came close to him and comforted him and told him to calm down. It was our decision to make. I want that also whatever you want, Jake. Whatever a father says, he says out of love and protective behavior and that decision is always right. If this love isn't meant to be completed then we should back-off.

(That could have ruined my revenge purpose, but now I was done hurting him. I couldn't hurt him as I was now really in love with him and after all what he said, I couldn't think right.)

He softly put his hands on my cheeks and said in loving tone, how can you say that? You already give up. Is this how much you love me? No! I know and feel how much you love me and you are saying all this just because you are afraid and want me to indulge in my Father's decisions as you say fathers are always right.

They might be right, but in love nothing is right except the love and relationship itself. See? I don't know anything, but what I do know is I need you always and forever. So, if you stop denying our destiny of being together, can I ask you for prom? Dance Ball!

My mouth drop open to hear whatever he said and was so soothing to the ears and my heart pumped fast. I couldn't help but fall in love more as my eyes poured down the tears.

He bends a little to reach me and then he kissed me and we made out. Then panting, I said in an excited way, yes! I will join you to prom, my gentle-man.

Jake jumped in happiness. After some time, he had to go. He left saying, so my lady, I will come around 7'O clock.

At night, he was going to pick me up for prom, the door bell rang; I checked the time, it was 6:30 p.m. I chuckled little to see how curious he was. I opened the door while doing some loving moves as I thought it must be Jake but no!

There was some guy wearing mask who entered within a blink of my eye, pushed me back and locked the door. Before I could call for help, he pointed gun towards me and said, I need silence and only answers from you! He draws the curtains to prevent someone to look inside.

I asked him, what he wanted; He sat right before me, looked right into my eyes and asked, So, Who are you? And how do you know Louka? To which I in not scared voice answered, so, who are you exactly, I assume you are the guy who stole my research and you are the one who send me threat mails?

He angrily said I am the one to ask questions here, not you! So, if you don't wanna get hurt, answer and I will leave. I answered, Hmmm, Interesting! You think, I will answer you? Then I have never seen such a stupid person like you whole my life! While I stressed word "LIFE" Ha!

So, you wouldn't let me go easy on you? Fine! He got up. Got hold of me, choked me and threatened me again.

Well! Obviously, I wasn't on this mission without preparation for such situations. I hit his balls as hard as I could! He let off of my neck and kept his hand there were I hit him. I rushed to kitchen and picked up round stick and went back to him. I kicked him, he fell on the ground. I attacked him from behind. Put the stick over his neck and choked him and asked questions like who he was working for? Who sent him here to investigate me? To which he answered, like! I will tell you.

Fine! I said. When the door bell rang! I again looked at the clock hanging on the wall; it was 6:55 p.m.

Hell! It must be Jake. I tried to think what should I do? I shouted Coming! Man said, so what now? Ha-ha! You are doomed! Either you can let me go or let Jake know!

I decided to let him go! I pulled him to the back door and threw him out, told him that I have a little message for whosoever you are working for or maybe I can say, Louka, tell him that your death is near, you are going to regret everything you did, tell him to stay away from Jake and his decisions and next time, please sent someone competent and I let him go!

The man looked at me with anger. It was clear, if for him, he would have killed me right there. So, I with confidence, closed the door on his face.

I hurriedly rushed to open the door, it was Jake. Hey! What took you so long to open the door?

I in a stammer tone, Oh! I wa-s in th-e b-athroom that's why!

As far as I could tell, he did believe me. He suggested that I should change as I was in pajamas. I went upstairs to change while he waited on the dining table.

After few minutes, Door bell again rang! I was accepting anyone. By the time I would have reached the door, Jake already was holding door knob to open the door.

I in suspicious way of speaking told Jake, let me see! He agreed with weird look. I opened half door and it was my uncle but his presence here was supposed to be hidden when everything was exposed about me. Couldn't risk! I told him to stay in hotel, will come there to see you. He handed me package and left.

Jake asked me who was at the door. I replied with, it was supposed to be a surprise! It's my package that I ordered. Now, I want you to close your eyes. To which he agreed. I went upstairs.

I was ready now, Jake gazed me for a while. He compliment me and we were off to prom where Nour and her new boyfriend, Sid joined us. We enjoyed a lot, Jake asked me for dance. We danced together on soft humming song. My phone ticked, it was a message from uncle. He wanted to meet me to plan next and he sent me the hotel name where he was staying. . As an excuse, I told Jake I was leaving as I wasn't feeling well! He whispered that he can come to drop me but I denied by saying I don't want to ruin your night, I'll be fine by myself. He unwillingly agreed and I left.

After walking for a while, I stopped cab and went to see my uncle. I reached the hotel named Hotel Check Inn. I knocked at the door, uncle opened up, I went inside. I hugged him. I told him everything that happened and we planned our next move. It took us an hour to decide effectively, when we were done, I was ready to do whatever it took.

I was walking towards my house when I saw someone sitting on the stairs of my house, it was dark, I couldn't tell from that far who was there! So, I decided go a little further and by tilting my head a little to see who he was, He was Jake. I shockingly started to come up with an excuse where I was? When he said, Erica? From past days, I think you are hiding something from me? Is it about my father? Did he do something? He can do anything to let his decisions work out? Or Is it about some guy? Are you dating someone else? I want answers? You are fooling me around? I thought we were more than this! But no! I was wrong. I love you and you are keeping secrets from me! You know, I never denied how and what I feel for you!

I tried to stop him, he told me to stay silent and let him talk. But I told him he was assuming everything that was completely wrong but he wouldn't listen! So, only way to stop him was:

I ran to him and held his neck bend it and kissed for a minute and then slowly backing off I told him to first listen to me and let me give my explanation and then he was free to decide but before that he can't decide by only considering his part of the story.

(In that moment, I just wanted to tell him everything but couldn't risk that.)

So, I told him that my uncle is here and I went to see him. Later at home, it was my uncle when I told you to let me see who was at the door. Now, before you ask any questions, let me clear that my uncle needs to stay hidden and why so? He has his own personal reasons. Now, you can speak!

Jake in confused voice, Okay! I trust you. I am sorry; I thought you were cheating on me! I couldn't help but scold you.

I in a satisfied voice, well! That shows and proves that you do love me and you are afraid to see me go! And you don't need to apologize! I should have told you before.

He held my hand, No! I should have understood your consequences or reasons. You have some rights of your own.

I replied, and from when our rights differentiated. Okay! Forget and let's get inside, its cold outside. I can make you a cup of coffee if you want?!

Yes, of course! I do want, Jake said.

We both went inside; I made him a cup of coffee. We talked hours and hours and then sad moment surrounded us when I told him maybe in few days, I guess something or everything could change, we wouldn't be same. He asked why I was assuming something like that.

(But he doesn't know the reality. The reality was how I saw his father, why was I in Romania? What were my intentions?)

So, I replied, I was saying just in case! If some day, the circumstances bring us in this situation where we couldn't believe each other or we can't face each other, please remember I love you and I will still love you no matter what happens in the future. All I know, is I need you here now and there where you can't stand by my side on your own will?

He was confused I could tell!

He expressed with confidence that he will be always there when I need him the most. He hugged and made me feel safe.

(But I knew the coming circumstances will turn him against me, even my love will be less for the same.)

I changed the topic by asking him random normal life questions.

He stayed all night. In the morning, I heard utensil noise that woke me up. I went downstairs to see what was happening. It was Jake trying to prepare breakfast, he was cooking pancakes.

I asked him in a surprised tone, you can cook? Life can't get any better! Ha-ha!

He replied laughing, Right. So, what do you

think? How do they look?

I nodding head, raised both eyebrows and said, Hmm! Let me see? And yeah Taste too!

He served me a plate with pancake. I took one bite and all I could have said about that pancake was "Heaven".

He chuckled a little and said thank you, Love.

I chuckled back while saying, you are incredibly awesome.

While we both were having breakfast, I decided to work my plan out.

(Inside my head, I was apologizing and was feeling sorry but couldn't help! I decided to tell him everything after it was done but by that time, he will know anyways.)

 So, I told him that I wanted to see his father in person. I want to clear few things before it's too late. As I added that I don't want him to question me regarding my decisions.

He agreed without denying single of my word. We went to college together; we were called perfect couple by everyone. I asked him, if he is planning future with me? To which he without giving any thought said, yes. Well! That made my day!

Next day was holiday, so, Jake decided to take me to see his father. I called uncle and told him I was executing my plan tomorrow. So, he wished me success.

Next morning, I went to see his father. We were outside Louka's office, I requested Jake to stay here while I entered the office alone.

Louka wasn't surprised to see me there! Louka said some things that really didn't chill me down the bones. He said, he was the one to threaten me by sending mails and messages and acknowledged that he even send his employee to my house to threaten me hard that whatever I was up to, drop the idea! He opened the drawer, took out my research on him and smashed it on the desk. You want revenge! Erica Raines, daughter of Adrian Raines. But will you tell me! You were just 9 when it all happened? How did you know any of this? I did research that you live with your granny in New York and No one else! Sure, that your grandma didn't knew anything! So, I am surprised to see you here in Romania dating my stepson. Well! Any of this is not a coincidence. It was your entire plan.

I stood there silently listening to him before taking any action; I wanted to listen to him, to his part in all this.

He continued so? Tell me! Before I call Cops to arrest you, go ahead!

Well! I replied, I just am here for revenge but before making a move, I want to listen to your part of story. Well! I was told, you were jealous of my father's, as you call it royalty so, my father's royalty. Was it all about this royalty, you didn't consider, Adrian has a daughter who was only 8; you didn't give it a thought that he has a mother to look after. No! All you thought about was all this royalty, money.

I remember, people teasing me that my parents were on run, they left you, for god knows what reason. Louka, you left a daughter wonder why her parents betrayed her but not for so long, I was only betrayed until I was in a position to understand and handle my consciousness.

That night when you visited me to tell you where time-machine was kept, I couldn't sleep all night and in the morning, when my parents didn't show up that day was like the day of reckoning for 8 year old. Now! After all the suffering you made us go through, give me one reasonable reason so I can spare your life.

By listening to that, Louka laughed like he was the devil of hell.

I couldn't really bear his stupid devilish laugh; I

took out my revolver and shoot both the bodyguards standing next to the door and then I said, if I have your serious attention when I was interrupted by Jake, he was probably scared to see bodyguards down with gun in my hand.

He addressed to his dad, what the hell? What's going on dad? Erica? Why are you holding gun?

Louka in worried tone, ordered Jake to stay back and don't involve himself in this.

I asked Louka, Wasn't his son worth knowing any of this? Well! I can't say further why you don't have your own kid! No wonder, it was your punishment from nature. What could have been better punishment for a person like you? No! You don't even deserve Stepson or Stepdaughter. You don't deserve anyone to be by your side when you die with regret and disgust. You ruined my life and you accepted to go everything right for you. Karma Louka karma does come around.

Jake again interrupted me while I was having conversation with his father. So, this time I caged my feelings, emotions and everything I felt for him.

(That was hard but had to do anyway)

Stood right before him and told him, if he dares to listen to the revenge story then who am I not to tell you and keep you away from the truth.

Louka shouted and begged me to keep Jake away from my evil intentions but he deserved the truth. I reached Louka and threatened him to tell Jake the mysterious story behind all his achievement, success and royalty?

Jake asked his father what I was talking about. He was innocent and confused at the same time as his father was being accused by his girl-friend for something he doesn't have any clue about.

To which I questioned, if you are not going to say, Louka! Then shall I proceed?

Louka in disgusted tone, it all started in New York.

I was colleague of Adrian, Erica's father. I was jealous of his royalty. That time Adrian was working on his time-machine, if that time machine worked, he could have made a fortune. Many times, to destroy and dirt his name and company, I did frauds and I was never caught cause Adrian could never have doubted me or accused me.

Jake shockingly stammered, WH-AT??? Tim-e

Mach-ine???

I told him to listen first then express and yet he had to listen to more of such things that can chill him to death.

Louka Continued,

So, I came up with a plan of destroying him, prove that he was in the run and steal his time-machine. In the morning, Adrian was home. I went to his company's cabin and stole the key of his home's secret drawer. It was the night of celebration for Adrian as it his companies 10th year anniversary. So, in my jealousy, I went to his house by the time he left for work, I went inside the house and searched for address or place where he hid the time-machine. I wasn't able to find the drawer. So, I scared Erica by saying that her parents were in danger and his father wants her to tell me where the secret drawer was. She trusted me as I spent a lot of time with her and her family all weekend and holidays, so she kinda trusted me with that. She showed me where the secret drawer was and also where the time-machine was kept hidden.

Adrian, his wife and his brother were celebrating while I was planning how to remove them from my path of success! When Erica's parents were returning from party, I

pretended like I was waiting for lift on Arizona Road. Adrian saw me and as normal, he offered me lift.

After sometime, we saw something in the middle of the road, it was something covered. I pulled out the revolver and put it on the head of Adrian and ordered him to pull over forcefully. I got out of the vehicle and reached the thing that was kept in between of the Arizona road. I uncovered it and it revealed Time Machine.

When Erica, your father tried to rationalize with me, he looked so helpless. He asked me even why I was doing what I was doing. I replied, you asking me? Obviously for your royalty! I want your position. You were stupid enough not to doubt me, it was me who tried to bankrupt your company; it was me who tried to dirt your company's name. So, let's get started with this and finish this as soon as possible! Your father stood there, without saying a word further, I could tell he was in shock! So! Without wasting few more minutes, I turned the time-machine on. Adrian at last spoke up, he said, he wasn't afraid of me but was afraid of the thought how his daughter that means you Erica will survive this? And for a minute, I was really caught in the emotions and felt did hit me but worked for one or two minutes only.

Jasper Raines, your uncle was so restless. If he was given the permission, he could have killed me right there but your father thought I was the person to be rationalized with. He was wrong. But what else could have they done? Nothing I presume! So, I had enough of emotional and mental torture and then I decided to carry my plan out.

I not only wanted to get Adrian's fame and money, but remove him. So, my plan was to use time-machine to get rid of him completely. I pointed my gun towards them so they are prohibited to stop me while I started setting timer on Time-Machine. When I was busy setting timer, your uncle Jasper decided to run away, so, he ran towards woods. I shot 2-3 bullets in his way, he fell, and definitely any of the bullets fired must hit him. One bullet hit his belly. He couldn't move an inch because he was hurt, blood all over there.

Getting back to Adrian, I set the timer on the date 25-10-2000, when Erica was born so they enjoy her birth each day. Then, I clicked the start button on the time-machine and I got your parents captured in the lapse of time on the date 25-10-2000. The time-machine roared and the clocks ticked fast and there, it was done. Now, when Adrian and his wife were gone from my sight like forever, I decided to finish my business with Jasper. When I reached where he fell but he was gone, he escaped. Now, it was serious issue that he could expose me and get me arrested. So, I went to his house and found out that he wasn't back yet. I waited all night, he didn't really show up and I could assume he died in the woods before reaching home.

After few days, it was out that your uncle was died and you had his funeral. It was clear that my way and crime remained unexposed as my last witness died. I moved to Romania right after I had everything of your father and lived happily ever after till the day I saw you, Erica, daughter of Adrian Raines dating or we can say, using my son to reach out to me, to the one killed your parents with time weapon.

Jake stood in shock listening to his father's crime; he couldn't really believe whatever he was saying. It was obviously, he spent his whole life with him, so, it would have been hard for him to accept the reality.

I listened to Louka's part of story, and replied with, how do you think I am here seeking revenge when your last witness died? How could have it even been possible to know your crimes that you were the person responsible, I was an orphan, that proved to the world that my parents were on run and they left me. So, here is the twist, my uncle didn't die that day, "The funeral held was fake" we faked his death. My uncle was home after few days, and he told us, he was treated by some-one who lived in the woods. How you betrayed my father. It was the same day; we held a fake funeral of my living uncle. He's been living under the shadows of his own and never had a chance to come by his own house and live happily and with freedom. He had to hide his existence just because of today and the revenge. After all is done, he will be free to stay at his home with his mother and niece. Ok! Leave this. My uncle is here in Romania, he's been helping me all this time. Now, without dealing further, I want you to tell me where is the Time-Machine?

Louka eagerly said that's not possible, I investigated about you few days ago and came to know you only live with your grandma. And yeah! I will never tell you where time-machine is?

I replied with confidence, his existence was hidden from everyone. No-one knew he survived that night. Now,

I reached him, squeezed his faced and put revolver inside his mouth, and said in angry tone, don't try me with this? I have lost everything, and now it doesn't matter to me if I have to go to jail for killing you.

I backed off, shot his leg and he shouted in pain and agreed to reveal the place where he kept the time-machine.

Louka took us to the warehouse, where he kept the time machine and I called uncle to reach there. After sometime uncle came there and he holds Louka by his collar when he was stopped by Jake and he said, it's not the right time for all this! We should let cops deal with him.

We all entered the warehouse, turned on the lights and in the middle of the room was time-machine. Jake and I were in shock to see my father's creation. So, I asked Louka, if he thought that this time-machine could have made a fortune then why didn't he did made that fortune? To which he replied I could have! But I didn't because it could have exposed me and for it to work, I had to release your parents in the first place, I could have done that, killed your parents as no one could have searched for them. But that's not how it works!

 I asked desperately what he meant. How does it work?
To which he didn't replied and left us in suspense. Then uncle answered that chilled me down the bones and left me thinking! He said when person/persons who are stuck in time are released, someone has to replace him and

that someone must be who released them.

Uncle turned the time-machine on, and carefully set the timer for the date 25-10-2000. As he pressed the button, an invisible force pushed us a little away. There! I saw my parents stuck and frozen. Seeing them like that was most painful moment of my life, they were turned pale and all my memories spent with them hit me. All I knew was setting them free at any cost.

I grabbed the manual book, and read it carefully to get some answers how to set them free? All conditions to be applied! And one of the page stated all what uncle said before:

"To set free the person frozen in time, you have to sacrifice someone in their place, if you do so, you only have 5 minutes left to take their position, if you don't do so, the person will be frozen back forever and it can be done twice only.

I asked Uncle why my dad kept such a condition in the first place, to which he replied with sadness, so that no one dares to use it in any sort of a way. This is a dangerous machine. See, it really restricted Louka from his evil intentions and prohibited to misuse the machine. It was the condition that halted Louka from destroying peace in the world. So, this condition was must.

I asked with intense eager to know, why didn't he use someone else to press the button and he could have stuck that person in time or he couldn't have needed anyone to replace my parents, he could have gotten them stuck forever by pressing the release button and not to replace?

Silence surrounded all of us as we were thinking the same, why? But then the awkward silence was broken by Louka. He said I got this idea. I did want to make money out of it. But I didn't follow the idea just because this time-machine was registered in Adrian's name, so I couldn't risk with that I could have been exposed, plus if I would have taken this thing over to use it, I had to undo all what was done with the machine and free the person stuck as I already said. After Adrian, I received his everything not this Time-Machine just because it was his own invention so, no one was subjected it as a matter of fact. If I took time machine out to make fortune, I would have been asked questions about the condition, because the time-machine displays whatever was done with it like history. So, it would have made them know it's used once. This machine was yet to be tested when I got Adrian and his wife stuck in time and really didn't knew the conditions then I would have used some other way but after it was done, it was done! I couldn't change any of this, so I let it be. Although, I was only trusted person left to handle Adrian's company and all other dealings as his daughter was only 8 and his mother old. So, I took over his everything. I had bank balance, cars and fame and then, I left New York. But not everything, it was declared in the agreement that I signed was after Erica Raines is 18 years old, all his father's achievement will transfer to her leaving me with only 20% of it. It meant I was the servant to protect his achievement. Nah! I wouldn't let that happen. So, it took me years to overcome this agreement. I stole the agreement from Erica's home. So, that helped me to transfer all the achievement to myself and I was successful in doing that by bad and good means.

Then, when Adrian went missing like he never existed, cops questioned me about time-machine as they wanted to take into their custody, as everyone in town knew Adrian's project of creating time-machine. He wanted to use it for future predictions, so we could have reversed the future of destruction and avoided many disasters. So, he working on creating time-machine was known to almost everyone. When cops asked me about the time-machine, I told them, he never mentioned to me where the time-machine was kept.

Jasper slapped him for his sins. Jake as his son couldn't stand any of this but also could have done nothing else. I was reading manual to see if there was any other way. None of us were in their minds, so no one was able think logically and come up with better options. Panic surrounded us.

Then as a loving daughter, I accepted to be sacrificed in their place. To which no one agreed not my uncle, not Jake and deep down I also didn't wanted to sacrifice myself just because I was getting my parents after a long period of time, didn't wanted to ruin it. But in spite of everything, I couldn't sacrifice any other innocent life. So, I came up with the idea.

I was restless, my heart was not in peace, and it was aching by the sight of my parents. All I knew was that I have to save my parents.

While everyone was busy denying my decision, I wasn't able to see my parents stuck there, it was painful. I aggressively rushed to time-machine and tapped on the button to set them free. Uncle and Jake shouted, No! No! Erica! No!

After few flashes coming out of time-machine and the clocks on it circled at high speed, after few sounds, my parents were free; they were moving and were alive. I rushed to them and hugged them as hard as I could and told them I was their daughter, Erica. They looked at me with an unavoidable look. My mom kissed me so did dad. They asked me so many questions. I was just looking at them and crying.

I helped them to stand up, when my hand was

held by someone, it was Jake. He was apologizing for his father's intentions and expressed his love in such a beautiful way. He told,

Even, if this relationship wasn't real for you, Erica. But it was for me and still is. I love you, please don't leave me, I can't live without you. Believe me, please, my heart is aching. I am hurt, I want to be with you forever, please?! We can destroy this time-machine, right? Then everything will be fine.

To that, my uncle said, that can't happen. Destroying this will not do anything. It is a machine that is functioned to combine back when destroyed.

By hearing that, I started crying and in a saddened tone, I accepted that I loved him. In the beginning, it was for revenge but then I starting fall for you and by now, I completely am in love with you and I myself want to spent rest of my life with you. Maybe our paths will cross again, but for now, we were just till here. From now on, you are free to flirt, Heh! And move on with your life for that you have my permission. I love you too Jake and I am sorry I betrayed you, lied to you many times but now the reasons must be clear! Thank you, Jake. You and the days spent with you were incredibly Awesome and I wanted to live in those moments. It was supposed to end this way. Unfortunately, I did. Goodbye! Jake. I love you.

Uncle came close, hugged me and asked, why? Erica? Why not me? I could have done it? I just hugged him back and whispered to him that it was time for a family reunion and his freedom as I had mine.

We heard sound, only 50 Seconds left. Everyone in the room panicked. Dad nervously asked what about the machine? To which I replied I got this dad. Mom asked what I meant by that. So, I went and took their place right before the time-machine.

I wanted the moment of me going to be fun and less painful. So, I tried to crack a joke but that didn't end well. I curiously asked, dad? How you are so young and mom you look as gorgeous as always. Dad with tears in his eyes answered me because we were stuck in the same time for long period, so our body didn't grew any further and our mind was not able to release growth hormone.

Flashes of white bright light covered the room and there, I was frozen and captured by the time. It was nothing like frozen. As we know how powerful time is. It heals everything, changes almost everything. Well! I was stuck in a moment of my life where nothing healed and changed. My mind was sort of rewinding the memories of my birth. I could see my mom giving birth to me and I could see the pain she was going through and my dad by her side comforting Mom. I saw my mother's suffering and my father helpless. After few minutes, I was born. The happiness in the room was touching skies. My dad jumped with joy and sniff with relaxation while my mom was released of the pain, she saw me and burst into tears. Then, nurse put the baby that was me on my mom's chest. She looked at me like I was the precious thing she ever came across and had.

All of a sudden, the clock on the hospital wall ejected a sound like a roar; I looked up to it as it ticked anti-clockwise at high pace and after the coming of light, the moment ended. My mom was again suffering from the pain of birth. My dad trying to comfort her and then I was born. The time repeated itself. It was happening over and over again. I was trapped in this moment for how long Gods know. Well! That sucked for me. I couldn't complain. It was my choice. I made this decision of being trapped in the same moment. To reduce the pain, I tried to remember other happy moments of life like my parents were alive now, moments shared with Jake, college days, childhood and all But No! Couldn't recall any of the memories but suffer the memory I was in.

I couldn't stop questioning myself; will anybody be able to save me after all the tragedies and illogical decision? I didn't have any hope of being rescued.

Back to the present life where everyone was sad to see me go. After me, Uncle called cops to deal with Louka. My parents were still confused what to do next to save me while Jake went to the place I was standing and cried. Door opens and cops were standing there, my uncle narrated everything, so they needed witness from outside, so Jake confronted to them and said that his step-father is behind every crime. He acknowledged that I being the witness want Louka to be punished for his sins. Then the cops arrested Louka for various committed crimes.

After months, my father and uncle came up with the idea of saving me. The idea was just plotted and yet to be done while Jake was ruined. He also lost everything. He pretended that he was happy, enjoying and living his life nicely. In college, he told everyone that Erica is never coming back, she's gone. He ruined himself after me, he couldn't handle himself after all what happened in past. Then a girl found him laying drunk next to the Milton hotel where Erica was staying, she picked him up, supported him and dealt with his miserable situation. She was Millie. She helped him to think rationally. She really was kind and cared. It felt like she was his guardian angel. She handled him like no one would have and made him believe that giving up is not the solution. If you and Erica were really heavenly made soul mates then this relationship will be completed. It will find a way; I have never seen such a sad ending, or no! It's not the ending. You still can get her just think correctly.

When Jake realized, he was doing everything wrong. The way he was, Erica would have never wanted me to be that way. He decided to visit my father after he believed that he couldn't live like that with the guilt of his father, thought of losing me for forever and continue ruining himself. Then he came up with the decision of helping my father with whatever plan he had.

From next day, dad, uncle and Jake all worked together. They used to shout at each other, arguing and all.

Now what will I tell you about myself. I was stuck in the same moment god knows for how much more time. I couldn't feel anything. I felt like I am the air flying and stuck in same time of 15 minutes. I felt like a molecule that feels nothing, doesn't grow, and doesn't digest, just there watching myself giving birth over and over again.

It took them months, to come up with the time watch idea that could take back 6 months we can call it flaw yet 6 months meant more than enough for them. It took them weeks to prepare, test the watch and connect it with the time machine. Now, it was ready! They couldn't wait to release me from the claws of time. They came up with the idea that can completely free me and no one has to do replacement.

(How? You'll see)

Jake was ready to use time-watch to go back 6 months to the day when it was my first day in Weinberg college. So, dad on the time machine tapped the button so did Jake on the watch and BOOM!!!

Jake was surrounded by the white light, then realized he was being teleported to the date 02/05/2019, 7:45 a.m.

When Jake opened his eyes and finds himself in

his room at his stepfather's Villa. Jake looks around, he picks up the phone and checks the date and day. It was Monday; 02/05/2019, 7.45a.m. With surprise, he yells with delight, yes!!! He couldn't resist the urge to see me, so he rushed as fast as he could to see me in the college.

He reached early. He took sit, was gazing outside the window and was lost with the thought what to do next. Erica enters the room, saw him gazing outside the window and when Erica was asked to introduce herself, I saw her with tears about to burst out, at that moment, all I wanted to do was get up, hug her and kiss her and share whatever he got through. But she doesn't know any of this. She looked confused by my weird personality and tears in my eyes. I took out paper and logically did some calculations about time, figuring out how to complete the goal.

After OR class, Jake left for the warehouse where he kept the time-machine. He reached thc place and connects pen drive to reset the time-machine's programs to allow him to use the time-machine according to the plan.

Flashback!

He remembers what Adrian told him to do

when he inserts the pen drive to upload the software.

Adrian in serious tone, so when you insert this pen drive, time-machine will reset some of its programs with the software in the pen drive. Be careful, it can release invisible force, so stay back right after you insert the drive. After the process is done, time-machine will allow you to change it and next, you know what to do!

Present time, Jake inserts the drive and runs away from time-machine. Machine starts to release forces and light for almost some time. Now the time-machine can be put into use. As the time-machine was displaying used once, can be used again only once. He sets the timer for 25/10/2000 the same day when Louka got Erica's parent trapped into the claws of time and pushes the button on time-machine and suddenly, white light again covered him, he fell on the road and checked time- watch. He had half an hour time to finish business here. He tries to rationalize where he was but couldn't understand when he saw a car coming from left side. He hides himself behind the tree in the woods and continuously gazes the car. By the time, car passes by; he sees his father holding gun pointed towards the driver.

 That's it, it's Arizona Road, he aggressively

expressed. He chased them. After he reaches panting and gasping where they were, his father already was standing next to the time-machine having conversation with Adrian about his position and money. He waits for the right moment to sneak in. Jasper runs towards the woods to escape, few seconds passed, bullet was shot, and he in shock saw my Jasper (uncle) fall. He walks steadily towards him and helps him to hide when he was hurt because of the bullet. Jake decides to flank right and attack Louka from behind. He flanks according to the plan framed by him and now, Louka was about to trap Adrian and his wife when Jake jumps, gets hold of his father and they starting fighting.

Jake shouts to Adrian in worried tone to turn the time-machine off. Adrian rushes and shuts off the machine. Jake struggles to hold Louka back and tried to rationalize with him that if he does this today, if he successfully gets Adrian and his wife captured in time, he will never have his own kids, he will never find peace after tonight.

Both he was more into the greedy self and could have done anything to accomplish his mission. Adrian reaches him while Jessica (Erica's Mom) goes for Jasper. Adrian picks up the gun, shot blow. Louka shouted in pain, bullet went through his leg. Adrian rushed to car, searched for mobile phone and called cops and ambulance.

Jake rolled up his sleeve, raised his left hand bit close to his eye and checked the time watch how much time was left before he was teleported back, even less than One min. Adrian surprisingly said you are from future! Who are you?

Jake opened his mouth to answer; he wasn't able to say his name! Except he said in alas! Obviously the future isn't the same, after today, it has changed so is my name and I am no longer stepson of Louka.

Bright light covered Jake and he was teleported back.

After Jake went back, Cops with ambulance accompanied them. They didn't talk about the boy who saved them. Uncle was admitted to hospital. After Louka was discharged from hospital, he will be directly sent behind the bars.

All Adrian and Jessica immediately rushed home and searched for Erica.

Erica was home safe obviously, they lived

happily ever after. But nothing was right in future or the real time.

Jake was teleported back to the warehouse on Monday 02/05/2019. Time-machine wasn't there. He assumed the time-machine must be kept back where it was supposed to be, where Adrian hid it. He used the Time-watch to go front 6 months to actual real time, he went down the white light and there he was the back in his time.

When he opened his eyes, he was expecting Adrian and Jasper there but he was sitting there again alone and the time machine was also missing. He went out trying to figure out what actually happened. He takes out his phone, he dials Dad. His dad picks up; he asks him what my name was? To which his father with laugh teased and said your name is James Serguis, son.

He was somewhere happy to hear Serguis again. He wanted to know everything and get logic out of all this but also didn't want to look like fool, so he decided to meet his father. When he reached his father's place, this time he was his own biological father, Louka Serguis. He assumed nothing much changed. He curiously asked his father, how he earned money, doesn't he remember me before I was his son? What happened after you were in jail? To which he replied, how did you know I was in jail? Well! I will not lie to you. I tried to sort of killing someone; I attempted murder that's why. My real home was in New York, after I was done with sentence, I moved here to make a fortune with loyalty and honesty, so did I.

Now, something heartbreaking hit him, he thought of Erica. He logically figured out that Erica must be in her real home in New York. So, He booked the ticket to go there. Available ticket was next day in the noon.

Now, he had so many things yet to understand about his before real father, what happened to him. He went to see for him and in before life he died, he was dead too in this time but this time there was a twist James came to know that his old father never had a child.

He in accepting tone, Okay!! It fits completely. He let me die when Louka took me over. So, it was better he never had a child. Well! God figured that out well.

Now, he thought I should ask Nour, what she has to say.

Next day, he decided to go to college. When he saw Nour by the side of football court, he curiously reached her and asked in doubt if she knew any girl named Erica or does any Erica studies here?

Nour answers in doubtful way that she doesn't know any Erica. James accepted that with no questions. Well! It was obvious that she doesn't know Erica after the future has changed.

Nour burst into laugh and asked if he was serious? Then she added Of course! Yes I know Erica and she's my best-friend and your girlfriend who joined Weinberg College past few months, I was messing with you, Ha! She punches James. And then asks worriedly, were you serious? You don't remember? What's wrong with you? You really forgot again? Did you? Nour now was a little worried about James forgetting state lately.

James couldn't understand! He desperately asked Nour, what she meant.

Nour in a worried tone, well! Once a day you forget Erica. You just saw her the day before; she introduced herself while you were gazing her sort of. You were on leave for some days because you were sick. Then the Day you showed up, we were talking, you approached us and you really didn't recognize Erica. We thought maybe you were sick enough to remember her.

James thought, Of course! It was the day, when I first saw Erica and it was the same day, when I was teleported, so maybe yes that's the reason why I didn't recognize her because the memories of the day were removed as I went back, then I fell sick obviously. Now, it all makes sense.

Nour shook him, James? Are you alright? You spaced out! Is something bothering you?

James couldn't wait any further. He asked her, where Erica was? Nour answered that few days back she just left, I don't know. I called her many times before, she didn't pick up. Later yesterday, she called with some different country number. She was happy and said I don't feel this much alive before. I couldn't understand. She stopped and questioned James; didn't you tell us that she was not coming back? She's gone! Well! You Duffer! She just went to her home to pay her parents a visit nothing serious as you described, and you made it look like she was I don't know, really gone! Obviously, I scolded her for disappearing like that and not let her best-friend know.

James jumped with joy and in excited voice, he asked she coming back? Just tell me already! Did she say anything about coming back?

Nour smiled and in happy voice, she said, she has really serious explanation to give, obviously to us but more importantly to the college authorities as she was gone for almost a year. So, she is coming back tomorrow noon. She sounded very excited to meet you, James like it was the first time. I am happy she is coming back.

So am I, Nour. More than anyone, James expressed with delight and impatience.

Next day, Nour and James went to pick up, Erica from the air-port.

Nour was happy to see Erica. She hugged her and scolded at the same time for leaving without telling them. Erica glanced at James and promised her that she won't do such things again ever. She handed her a box and said it's for you and you can't even give it a thought, how much I missed you and yeah your talks! I missed everything.

James stood there, he wasn't literally saying anything. She hugged him and whispered, dad told me to tell you that it worked!

James hugged back as tight as he could after remembering heartbreaking separation and suffering he got afterwards. Nour also felt peace, safe and comforted James by saying; it's done now I am here with you, right? And I promise I am not going anywhere this time.

Erica took car keys from James. I'll drive. We all got in the car and went to the restaurant to have lunch.

Erica looked at James desperately and in excited tone asked so? James? Not really much different from Jake and who is your father? Nour laughed, what are you guys talking about?

James answered Erica with something that she couldn't digest and she shouted what? You are a Serguis? Okay! And Louka is your father? Gee! Duh!

Nour shockingly asked Erica that she also doesn't remember her boyfriend's parents?

James and Erica shared eyes. They reached restaurant. Nour went straight to washroom. James was now worried about whatever happened after the day he was back. Almost everything changed; they were living different lives before. He expressed that I am no longer Jake Winslow there have been character switch. I am James Serguis and you are Erica Raines whose parents are alive now. My old dad never had a child. My father is Louka Serguis; all my thoughts were driving me crazy!

Erica tried to comfort him by saying; it was to be this way. Your name just changed not your character. What's the difference you being Louka's son than being his step-son, anyways you ended up being his son and for me, it was my decision to save my parents from jaws of time. And you can't even imagine what I got through. I felt nothing, all I felt was I was kind of molecule stuck in same time seeing myself being born all over and over. Now, forget everything. We have to help each other to get through this. It's God himself who helped us in the first place, it might have gone wrong or might have not worked. We could have ended up dead who knows. I want you to look into my eyes, I need you, it's hard to go through all this but for me it's harder.

I really didn't wanted to tell you this now and ruin the moment but you left me with no other option there's this thing, I am having terrible nightmares that I can't bear anymore. So, as much as you want me by your side, I want more than that much.

Waiter brought us the dinner after some silent moment, Nour companied us back. We had lunch and Nour decided to put homecoming welcome party, we talked, laughed and enjoyed to the fullest while we had a lot to discuss yet and then we were off. We dropped Nour in our way back and both of us headed to my hotel. James started with the left over conversation and he promised to be there with me each time I suffer.

James with suspense asked why nightmares? You parents were also stuck in time? They just did fine. To that, Erica replied with surprise, the time wasn't meant for me. I was being born that time so I was there but as a baby, but when I got stuck, I was seeing everything, my mom, dad, the baby and the doctors that I wasn't meant to see. Now, each night, I saw myself trapped in that moment and feel pain and suffering. Maybe it was my part in all this. Nightmares feel real. Mom helped me to go through these days now it's something that's a little different, it doesn't feel that real now but somewhere it still does. Mom didn't wanted me to come back but I had my life and I needed to get on with it, that's why I am here to start a new life with you, and forget all the pain, sufferings.

James helped me to go through my nightmares while I helped him go through his. We accepted our fates. We loved each other more and more every single day. James was selected as the captain of football team; I was always there to support him. We graduated from Weinberg College and then on my birthday, James decided to go for something that every girl dreamt of.

Right in front of all who had come for celebrating my birthday, he kneeled down, pulled out the ring and proposed,

Marry me Erica "I love you!!! I will do all my best to keep you happy. I promise to stay by your side no matter what. I take oath that I will protect you by any means. Please love, accept my marriage proposal.

Erica's eyes were filled with tears about to pour down as she accepted his proposal and added that she also promises to stay by his side, protect him, love him more and more and keep him happy for the rest of his life.

Now, you can imagine what happened next, right? They got married and lived happily ever after. Now all of us know when the ending is not happy, it's not the ending and in this story it was not only happy but complete.

Thank you for READING!

ABOUT THE AUTHOR

The story is penned down by Noureen Jan. It's her first short story, in spite of writing short stories; she's been working on her upcoming novel and has already uploaded many heart touching poems. She is passionate and looking forward to become professional Writer. It was her dream to write and publish in her name, so this story is proof that she can do anything.

About studies, currently pursuing IMBA (Integrated Masters of Business Administration) from University of Kashmir. She manages both her dreams and studies efficiently, so that she can balance and carry out each work important to her.

To know more about her, always follow her on Instagram @Eternal_Author_ (Pen Name) and for working queries, just email on noureenjan2@gmail.com